July '23

"Dear
do

Written by
Sharon Blyth

To the Best Dad!

Hope you find much joy in these pages.

All my love
Sharon
x

ISBN: 978-1-916596-91-7

Foreword

All profits from this book will be given to The Love Moldova Foundation www.lovemoldova.foundation
Love Moldova is seeking to eradicate poverty and relieve suffering of those most vulnerable in Moldova.
Improving life experiences through loving support, education and practical help; bringing hope to the hopeless through the "Good News" of Jesus.

This is **little book of BIG miracles** is written to encourage and build up those who are weary. To remind us that God always has and always will perform His miracles. He doesn't change, He is the same yesterday, today and forever.

My memoire is a testament to His continuous goodness, constant care and overwhelming kindness. My experience is summed up in the lyrics from this beautiful song from Bethel Church Redding California.

I love You, Lord
Oh, Your mercy never failed me
All my days, I've been held in Your hands
From the moment that I wake up
Until I lay my head
Oh, I will sing of the goodness of God
And all my life You have been faithful
And all my life You have been so, so good
With every breath that I am able
Oh, I will sing of the goodness of God

Dedications

To my wonderful husband Bill, without whom this book would not have been achieved. Thank you for your patience, for all your encouragements and for rooting for me and cheering me on to the finish line. You're the best!
To our incredible blended family whom we love beyond measure, treasure and believe in, we enjoy every encounter with you, thank you for loving us back.
Samantha and Leo
Andrew and Rachelle
Helen and Michael
Kate, Paul

When I wrote this short memoire, it was, I felt my legacy to our grandchildren and a wonderful demonstration of how "Love Never Fails"
So, to Evelina, Francesca, Tom, Benjamin,
Holly, Owen and Joseph.
We love you more than words can say and we pray that you will have much joy as you turn these pages.

Know that you are loved, now and always,
just as you are!
Grammy Sharon

Chapter 1

"I Want That One!"

As I stared into a sea of faces, I dreamed of meeting 'the one!' Which one would be mine? A wonderful glow of excitement was in the pit of my stomach, and a smile spread across my face as I pondered and studied each image.

But then, there he was. A face full of kindness, gentleness, nice looking, relaxed, confident, and for once, on reading his profile, he was not looking for a lady 20 years his junior!

I was praying, is this the one, is he right for me? I felt convinced just soaking in his image that Bill was THE ONE! He almost jumped off the page and into my heart.

So, what happens now? Do I message him? Do I pray that he will be in touch with me if he's right? How should one approach these situations? I was way out of practise. Then the miracle began to unfold. That same evening, whilst contemplating my next move, I received an email from Bill asking if I would consider meeting him for coffee. I liked his gentle approach. The email began, "If I may be so bold ...." I liked that very much, gentle, unassuming, already experiencing a feeling of confirmation that he was a good choice. But let's not get ahead of ourselves here.

We must remember that there are hundreds of people on this particular Internet dating site, all hoping to be picked, all searching profiles for the one! So, to be picked out just as I was looking at Bill's particular image was a miracle in itself!

However, I wanted to be absolutely sure; I needed God's guidance and affirmation that this was the right chap for me. So, I prayed, "Father, if this is right, please, can he be wearing a dark blue woollen overcoat when we meet?" You may be thinking that this was a strange request, but you see, I don't do anoraks and felt that any man worth considering should make the effort and turn up really smart, suited and booted as it were.

It was also a tactical prayer that gave God scope to intervene and assure me that I was doing the right thing. And so, we arranged to meet at Reading station for coffee at 10 am Monday, 30th November 2015.

This is how the miracle began... Just a few days earlier, I had registered with Christian Connections, and here I was, heading for my first encounter with a man!

I couldn't have stepped into this dating realm without the sound encouragement and advice I had received, courtesy of a team at Holy Trinity Brompton Church in Kensington.

You see, I had attended their really helpful course called Restored Lives. It was a course for people either going through a divorce or were already divorced or even in the stages of separation. It was truly liberating and, to my surprise, showed me over the course of eight weeks that there was much that I hadn't dealt with since my divorce nine years previously.

Week eight was a celebratory dinner, and candidates could share all that was good and how each of us had moved on, had benefitted, and had been encouraged by our course facilitators. I was sitting beside a facilitator from our group called Peter, a retired police officer. Peter was accompanied by his wife, who, following his divorce a few years before, he had met this lovely new life partner on Christian Connections, a dating website for those aligned with the Christian Faith.

During the course of the conversation that evening, Peter suggested that if I felt ready for someone new in my life, then maybe I should give it a try. So, I did! The very next evening, I registered on the site and posted up my profile. I experienced many mixed feelings, my emotions seesawing from excitement to anticipation to feelings of vulnerability. Would

I be liked, would anyone contact me, how does it all work, am I doing the right thing, etc., etc.??

I later discovered that Bill had been encouraged to join a dating site by a friend who simply said, "Bill, you research and find everything else on websites; why not search for a new partner on a dating website?!" I later discovered that he had registered with Christian Connections on the same evening I had and was equally nervous!

Even more surprising was the fact that I had just returned home from serving in Eastern Europe, in a small country called Moldova, where I had spent the last nine years. I was taking a six week break to spend Christmas with my family in the UK.

That all began in 2006; I was really struggling with my painful divorce and God very clearly called me to serve in Moldova. I will share this miracle with you later in the book, but for now, let's get back to coffee with William (Bill) Blyth.

Back to the story … I journeyed from Bath that morning, having spent the weekend with my brother and sister-in-law. We had discussed Bill's photograph and decided that his image was just right. On reading his profile, I discovered that he was an engineer, a problem solver. He was widowed, had a family and grandchildren, and, most importantly, he was tall! I had always wanted a tall man to look up to. I, too, was a mum of three amazing adults and had three grandchildren then, now 4.

My excitement grew with every station we passed through; the butterflies in my stomach were a delight, and the thought of an exciting encounter with a stranger was a fantastic feeling.

We had arranged to meet at the bottom of the escalator on the platform. Having never been to Reading Station before, Bill informed me that it was vast and easy to miss each other, so this seemed like a sensible solution. However, when Bill arrived, he discovered that there were two escalator staircases, one at each end of a very long platform, and he had to choose one of them as the train pulled into the station.

To our utter amazement, when the train came to a halt, my carriage door opened, and standing directly in front of the door at the bottom of one of the escalators was Bill! What were the chances of that?! My train from Bath had at least ten carriages! Even more miraculous, he was wearing a dark blue woollen overcoat and the biggest smile! I was not disappointed!

Of course, Bill had no idea of my conversation with God, but I knew the minute I saw him that this would be a life encounter, not just coffee.

We chatted for more than two hours, neither of us conscious of the time and all the time we were talking I kept looking at his mouth thinking, I could kiss those lips! A very important factor in my book was to find kissable lips, a tall, handsome chap but most of all kind, gentle and smart.

Bill was all of the above and much, much more. Within nine months, we were married and living in Camberley.

How good is our God! If we ask Him for His intervention, for His decision-making in our lives, we have nothing to fear. He always comes through, the God of the miraculous!

We are now seven years into our marriage and are totally complimentary in our skill set. The skills I lack are amply provided by Bill, and the skills he lacks, are likewise provided by me.

It was very important to me that Bill would also fall in love with Moldova, as this little nation had captured my heart. Bill visited Moldova in May 2016. He was introduced to some of my amazing friends there and was totally overwhelmed by their love and hospitality. It didn't take long for Moldova to get under his skin. Bill fell in love with the people and the nation of Moldova, and within a month, they had captured his heart.

We packed up my belongings; a suitcase of books and a suitcase of clothes; left my little gypsy caravan where I had been living in Moldova, and travelled home in a 4x4 across Europe, every part of our journey being an adventure.

O Happy Day" 3rd September 2016

God took me from a little caravan with no possessions into a beautiful four bedroomed detached house in Camberley. I felt that Bill was my knight in shining armour - a rags-to-riches story. However, the truth is actually, God was my knight in shining armour and masterminded the whole encounter. It surely was God's goodness and favour that won the day!

We are now founders of The Love Moldova Foundation and continue to visit and support the work, investing heavily in the lives of people, seeing Jesus honoured and people set free as they come to know more of His love for them.

Our lives are in God's hands; He knitted us together and gave us His blessing, and we are now looking forward to many, many happy years in His service.

Never doubt God's mighty power to work in you and accomplish all this. He will achieve infinitely more than your greatest request, your most unbelievable dream, and exceed your wildest imagination! He will outdo them all, for his miraculous power constantly energises you. Ephesians 3: 20 TPT

Chapter 2

God's Rescue Plan!

I just sat there motionless, both hands firmly grasping my seat cushion, watching the panicked and shocked expressions on the faces of the cabin crew. Their activity was frantic as they ran purposefully up and down the aisles of the plane. I was left in no doubt that this was a serious emergency!

The air began to fill with thick smoke, and my oxygen mask immediately appeared in front of my face having dropped from the panel above my head. Then it happened…

Suddenly the aircraft dropped from the sky as if the engines had stopped and we had lost altitude. I couldn't tell you how far exactly, but enough to lift me out of my seat and back down with a bump! My breakfast tray, which was now empty, clattered loudly as I watched croissants and coffee rolling down the aisle like a landslide.

I began to think, is this it? Am I about to die? Will I ever see my family again?

My thoughts, I am ashamed to recall, were that my brand-new black leather trench coat, which I loved, would be completely destroyed in the wreckage. I am embarrassed to share my shallow, selfish thoughts with you, but sadly, they are the truth.

I was feeling remarkably calm until I looked around at the passengers near me. On my left, in the seat opposite, across the aisle, was an elderly gentleman who was deathly pale, and I was convinced that he was no longer of this world. Then the children towards the back of the plane began to cry loudly. On my right was a gentleman sitting in the window seat, and I thought I would ask him if he would mind holding my hand as the plane, I feared, could crash land any minute!

I had just had that thought when the captain began to speak. We had been waiting for what seemed like an age for some information. A calm, steady voice began to relay just what had happened. One of the engines on the aircraft had blown, causing a fire that they had miraculously been able to extinguish. He reassured us that everything was now under control and that as we were very near Zaventem airport, Belgium, our destination, we would land with one engine!

The smoke began to clear, and composure slowly returned. The gentleman on my left seemed to regain his colour and, to my great relief, started to shuffle in his seat.

We landed safely, and everyone on board broke into spontaneous applause and cheering. We were so relieved to be on the ground, alive and unscathed.

It was the winter of 1997 when I experienced my dramatic “near-death encounter”. I was travelling to Brussels for business, a medical conference for which I was responsible as the Director of Bristol Myers Squibb College.

We were expecting 150 General Practitioners to attend the conference, which would be repeated over two consecutive weekends. I travelled a great deal in those days to many different countries and was very used to flying, but this was my very first experience of this kind! It was also the first time I checked into a hotel, ordered a large brandy at 10.00 am, and took to my bed for a couple of hours!

When I look back, I am not at all surprised that this strange encounter occurred during this time because what followed was to transform my life and was truly a miracle.

The very next weekend, as I was preparing for my final trip to Brussels, I received an unexpected telephone call from my brother, Eric. He asked me to attend his baptism service on 2nd November, which happened to be the final day of my 2nd conference in Brussels. Eric had previously spoken to me about his newfound faith, but I just thought that he had gone bonkers and was not remotely interested in what he had to say. So, you can imagine how relieved I was when I could honestly make my excuses and decline his invitation as I would be working on that day in Brussels and therefore couldn't possibly be there.

However, a few days passed, and I started to feel uneasy, guilty feelings creeping in. Mulling over the importance of this proposed event to Eric and the fact that we had no living relatives, I began to change my mind and think that maybe I should be supporting him in some way. So, reluctantly, I made arrangements to be able to fly home. I booked a flight for early on the Sunday morning, 2nd November, which enabled me to attend the service planned for that evening.

I left the hotel bright and early that day, around 7.00 am, checked into the club lounge, and helped myself to a lovely breakfast and steaming hot cup of coffee.

A few minutes into my delicious breakfast, the receptionist came to tell me that my flight had been cancelled and that the airport was fogbound, so the chances of flying out were very slim. I was almost relieved and ready to call the hotel to book a room for the night and make plans to fly home the following day, fog permitting.

However, before I had an opportunity to make that call, the receptionist returned to let me know that there was one flight to London, and as I had a fully flexible club ticket, I had been allocated a seat.

Darn it! Just when I thought I could back out, still feeling uncomfortable with the whole idea, I now had no choice; I just had to go.

That same evening, I found myself in a school hall in Leicester that was used by my brother's New Life church.

I was greeted many times by various people, all insisting on hugging me and telling me how much they had heard about me already. A very uncomfortable feeling of irritation began to cast a cloud on my mood, and I remembered thinking, if just one more person hugs me, I'm leaving!

Smiling through gritted teeth, I was ushered to my seat. Eric began to tell his story, the journey he had been through, of failed relationships, loneliness and despair. Lost, sad, and very alone, he had fallen on his knees and asked, "God, if you are there, will you please help me"? As a result of that cry for help, he talked of an immediate sensation of a physical hand on his shoulder and an audible voice that said, "Eric, I'm here for you; you don't have to do this on your own!"

As I listened to this incredible experience, the tears started rolling down my cheeks as I realised, for the first time, just how deeply unhappy and miserable my brother had been and that I had been so full of my own importance and lifestyle that I hadn't even noticed or been remotely interested.

Eric spoke of a peace that had filled him and a joy that he now has, and all the while, I am trying to make sense of the fact that God came physically and touched him. Wow! If I am honest, I guess I was a bit envious in a way, as I had never experienced a living God who cared so deeply that he would hear a small voice asking for help. What was that?!

As the service continued, there was much singing, beautiful words, and music, but I was so busy choking back the tears that I couldn't sing a word. What was happening to me?

I watched in wonder as the service unfolded and some people very gently started moving to the front for prayer. Each person that received prayer seemed to fall limply to the floor, caught in the arms of a helper who lowered them gently. They looked so full of peace, serene, as if they had experienced a touch from heaven. Intrigued and eyes wide open at this point, I watched with a hungry curiosity that seemed to pull me in.

I was thinking, I'm not sure what is happening here, but I want to experience it, that deep sense of peace and release that seemed to be filling everyone who received prayer.

At the end of the service, I was sitting in my chair mulling over the events of the evening and feeling that it shouldn't end. The service was over, but my questioning had just begun. What was the next move? Would I experience that intense sensation of peace if someone prayed for me? I asked Eric exactly that same question. He said he didn't know but would be happy to find someone to pray with me if that was what I wanted. And, to my surprise, it was exactly what I wanted.

It was then that Sam, a young church pastor, came and sat beside me. He could see my confusion and tears and also a sense of searching hunger for a new experience. Sam prayed with me and then bowled a googly when he said that I should ask Jesus to show me the way, to come into my life, to get myself right with God. I wasn't expecting that challenge and can remember feeling very hesitant as I searched for the words to say. To my amazement, I did it! I told God I was sorry that I had shut Him out, that I wanted Him in my life, I wanted to know Him and His precious peace. I committed my life to Him right there and then!

That's when it happened… my whole body became totally relaxed and filled with peace. I was sitting down so couldn't fall into anyone's arms, but I knew that something had entered the very depths of my soul, and I was at peace. Jesus painted a smile on my face in that moment, which has never left me. I felt I had finally come home and that I belonged to something far greater than I had ever imagined.

I felt accepted and released from all my cares. It was the most amazing and dramatic experience of my life!

Eric confessed later that he had been praying for me to become a follower of Jesus for the past six months and had prayed specifically for this to happen at his baptism service. Wow, the miraculous power of prayer.

I later reflected on my "near-death encounter" which had happened the weekend before; the fog which almost prevented my attendance at the service, and it was then that I realised that there was a force that was trying to stop me, a force that wanted me to be taken out so that I couldn't find my life in Jesus.

So, here's the thing; I wasn't looking for Jesus, but He was surely looking for me, and when He pursues you to follow Him, there is no force in heaven or on earth that can stop you from finding Him.

I was born again. I felt truly alive for the first time in my life. As a follower of Jesus for these past 22 years, I have enjoyed a full life of adventure and discovery, my cup always running over with blessings. If He can do that for me, who was a self-centred, ambitious, "up myself" and didn't care about anyone else type of person! He can do it for You!

I now fully understand what it is to have "life in all of its fullness".

Jesus said, "But I came to give life – life in all its fullness" John 10:10

My life began anew on 2nd November 1997, and I have never looked back. My past was wiped clean, and all of my guilt and shame were washed away by the blood of Jesus on the cross. My future was secured, and I was, at last, able to walk in total freedom.

Here is your ticket to freedom too… Why not ask the lord Jesus to come into your life by praying the prayer below? It will be the best decision you have ever made.

Dear Lord Jesus, Thank you for dying on the cross for my sin.
Please forgive me. Come into my life. I receive You as my Lord and Savior.
Now, help me to live for you the rest of this life. In the name of Jesus, I pray.
Amen.

Chapter 3

Divorce! Out of Adversity Comes Opportunity!

I didn't know it at the time, but I was about to be thrown into the greatest adventure of my life. I was broken and in immense emotional pain; my life was total confusion and despair. I thought I had lost everything. Pain, confusion, and disbelief were my constant companions.

It was the night my husband wanted to split! We had been married 31 years; maybe not the best marriage but certainly not the worst. We had encountered many challenges along the way, but never the less, I didn't think for one moment that we wouldn't grow old together. I always thought that marriage was for life.

If you are reading this and have had a similar experience of relationship breakdown or divorce, then you will understand the pain and devastation that ensues. The utter confusion of it all and the grieving of a life that has ended, life as a couple has just died.

It was in 2005/6 that I experienced immense loneliness; I felt completely alone for the first time in my 52 years. I had lost everything, my identity as a wife, running a family home, and all that is involved in that, now no longer a Mrs but not a Miss? I remember thinking what am I now? Who am I? How do you describe yourself in social circles when you are no longer two but one?

I had been in the position for 31 years, running a successful home and family, keeping everything together. We entertained, had many friends to stay, cared for our neighbours, and kept an open-door policy.

It was difficult to accept that I didn't have that home anymore. My role was no longer required; it had been taken by someone else. It wasn't helpful that the new woman in my shoes was not only 12 years younger than me but also a close family friend. I felt surplus to requirements, substandard, and just not good enough! Everything had been taken away from me.

I am the ex-wife of a man who is the father of my children. Point ends!

There is no way to fully describe the loneliness and confusion that I felt, and the pain was devastating at times!

"And once the storm is over, you won't remember how you made it through, how you managed to survive. You won't even be sure whether the storm is really over. But one thing is certain. When you come out of the storm, you

won't be the same person who walked in..." ~ Haruki Murakami.

This quote is so true, the storm rages, and time passes, and although it can be years rather than months to recovery, it does resolve, and the person that walks out of the storm is completely new.

As Jim Rohn would say, "For 6,000 years, Spring has followed Winter. It always does and always will!"

Whilst I was wrestling with my current circumstances and emotions, a friend asked me if I would go with her on holiday, a first for me, a girly holiday. This sounded like a lot of fun and just what I needed at that time.

We took off to a B&B in Watergate Bay, Cornwall. We had planned a five-day stay just to chill, relax and get some head space. I spent my mornings walking along a deserted beach surrounded by cliffs, and my friend Anita spent most of her days chatting on the telephone to her new-found boyfriend.

We would meet for coffee in the Watergate Bay Hotel around 10.30 am every day and decide how to spend the remainder of our day. It was just perfect; absolutely no pressure.

I used my deserted beach walks to cry out to God. I vented my feelings; I cried and shouted to the skies. I don't think I had fully appreciated how much anger I had stored up. I started to ask God for a purpose, what did He want of me? Where did He want me to go, be, do? What was I doing in this situation, and how was He going to rescue me from it?

One morning, I remember shouting to Him, I don't care what it is, just tell me, and I'll do it! I was so lost and alone on the inside that I just needed a goal, something to aim for, something that I could give myself to and would, in return, give me a reason to keep on, keeping on. God was silent!

A month later, I was having coffee with a friend, and we were discussing my experience in Watergate Bay. As we were chatting, I suddenly heard these words come out of my mouth, "What I really want to do is go to Moldova, live in a village, and learn the language," at which point my friend said, "Well, what's stopping you?"

That was it!!

You see, I had visited this tiny country in Eastern Europe on two occasions. I had an opportunity to join a group of people from my church for a mission trip to a small village called Risipeni.

Following my experience of Jesus, I was passionate about changing the world and jumped at the chance to visit a new culture and do some good. That was back in the summer of 1998.

In 2002, I was commissioned to lead a group of teenagers to the same village to deliver a very specific project. The village people were extremely poor and needed fresh milk to make butter and cheese, etc. We were asked to build a cow shed and provide a couple of cows for just that purpose.

The people of Moldova are wonderfully hospitable and sacrificed their own needs in order to provide for the team; they were so grateful. On our last day, we discovered that they had used their winter stock of chickens so that they could feed us. Their hearts were truly sacrificial, and it was very humbling for a group of young people from the West to experience such kindness. I know for sure that the young people were changed, challenged, and never the same again!

I had fallen in love with this little nation and felt strongly that someday I would go back. The Mission field was an exciting place where God seemed really up close and personal, and I liked that.

It suddenly felt so right in that moment as I was going through the trauma of divorce. I felt that I had been given an open door to pursue something new, to find myself again, and to explore all that God had in store for me. There seemed to be no better time. My children had all moved on, all in their 20s, and I no longer had a husband to care for or consider. I was a free agent.

However, the big questions began to dawn on me. How was a mature woman going to walk away from her full-time position, up sticks, and move to Moldova with no money to do so? I had no language under my belt and nowhere to live. My hope was that a family might take me in as their lodger initially, and I would work out the rest as I went along. After all, if God was truly in this, then I didn't need to worry about a thing; I just needed to step out!

I was working for a Christian Youth Organisation at the time of my divorce called Crusaders. My boss at that time was amazingly supportive. He had watched my journey through separation and divorce; he had seen my distress and, at times, despair and had pledged to help me, whatever it took to get me back on track.

Matt and the leadership team were an amazing support. We had a long chat about the possibility of moving out to Moldova more permanently and agreed that I should take a sabbatical for three months. I was to go on an extended visit to Moldova, from February through to May, and if I still felt that this was the right thing to do, then the team would assist me all the way.

I was to write a report of my stay and my achievements whilst out there and to feed that back to the team in the UK.

Needless to say, my experience was incredibly exciting; I was learning a new language, I was deep into my bible, reading through the New Testament in three different translations, and also learning to touch type.

I loved the culture, living with a beautiful family in Risipeni, and getting my head around a whole new me. I'm sure that I got many things wrong, but ignorance is bliss, as they say, and people were so gracious that nothing came back to my ears. I wouldn't have understood what they were saying anyway, as my language was still developing.

I returned to the UK from Moldova in mid-May and reported back to the leadership team that I felt this was a definite God call on my life. It was agreed that I would work my six months' notice and move to Moldova in February 2007.

My church family and friends were incredible, and it wasn't long before I had lots of support. Whenever I shared the call on my life and what I was about to do, I was blessed in abundance. I needn't have worried about finances or a family to stay with, everything just fell into place, and I had been blessed with enough financial support to cover all my expenses and my digs.

I left Crusaders in 2007 with more than two months' salary through gifts and personal support; people were so very kind.

Everything that I needed had been miraculously provided.

I lived and worked in Moldova for three years; I served the elderly population of the village who were desperately poor, sad and very lonely.

Thanks to my church, we had raised enough funding to turn a derelict building into a community home for elderly grannies whom I loved. God sent me supernatural love for these old ladies whose stories would break your heart.

This beautiful home for grannies is called Casa Helen, and the building and provision for that was indeed another miracle. Suffice to say, at this stage in my story, we have 22 beds, 5 carers, a manager, an accountant, and a man who does all the heavy chores like lighting the fire and stoking the boiler.

I will come back to this topic in a later chapter and describe the many miracles that we experienced in the village. Also, to recount some of the stories that the ladies shared of their past. Rearing children in a harsh communist totalitarian state. Living in a village with no running water, no heating other than a wood burner, growing their own crops, and raising a few chickens to stay alive. They often had 7,8,9,10, or more children!

Background

However, the economy in Moldova was very bleak; the nation had gained independence from a communist state in the early 90s, but the people had no experience of democracy, competitive trading, etc. They had lived in small co-operatives, all working the land for the same salary, same living conditions, and no room for entrepreneurial spirits or for exercising fresh vision. There was no vision.

Proverbs 29:18, KJV Where there is no vision, the people perish.

Families were hungry with no or extremely low incomes. The men had become demoralised, no longer able to care and provide for their families, and many had turned to alcohol to drown their sorrows. According to official data, there are over 30 thousand alcoholics in Moldova. There are about ten undisclosed addicts for every registered one. These numbers increase year in year out. Doctors believe this to be the result of social and economic factors. Many grow despondent about their future and take to drink.

Many men had fled the country to find work in Moscow; some had gone to Greece, and some to Turkey and other European countries. Families were suddenly without fathers, and sometimes both parents had left. The children, if they were fortunate, were left in the care of their grandparents however, many were left alone. Sometimes a kindly neighbour would look in on them. The older children, often just nine or ten years old, taking care of the babies. There were many tragic stories of abandonment and often parents not returning home!

Family structures began to break down, and this left two ends of the social spectrum extremely vulnerable, the very young at one end and the very old at the other. Orphanages filled up quickly with abandoned children, and the elderly were left to fend for themselves in extremely harsh conditions.

There was no/little social care or government funding available.

It seemed timely then that the God-given vision for Casa Helen should be realised and a strategy developed to provide a beautiful communal home for the abandoned elderly.

Chapter 4

The Miracle that was Casa Helen

Winter had most definitely arrived! The snow was knee-deep, shimmering crystal, and the view from my window across a small valley was breath-taking. It was the end of 2008, and I was living at the top of a derelict building that my church fellowship had purchased in the hope of establishing a youth centre in the village.

The second floor had been refurbished, and I had two rooms. I made one of the rooms a bedsit as it was so cold, and economically, it was much more sensible to heat just one room. It was a safe haven where I felt completely at peace with the world.

I had a small Belling tabletop cooker with two electric plates; a sink unit which wasn't plumbed in but had a bucket of clean water from the well for drinking and an empty bucket to catch the slops underneath the drainage hole of the sink, all beautifully hidden in the sink unit cupboard. I slept on a sofa bed and had a small oil-filled radiator to heat the room. It was my space, and I felt cosy and safe in it.

However, it grew cold, and temperatures often plummeted to $-30_{o}C$ that winter and my small, oil-filled radiator somehow didn't "cut

it!”
My beautiful daughter, Kate, became concerned for my welfare as when we occasionally chatted on Skype, she could see the vapour of my breath and my red, cold nose. So, Kate sent me a wonderful gift that would keep me warm whatever the temperature; it was called a SELK! This is a padded space suit with a hood that can keep you warm at extreme temperatures. It was like wearing a sleeping bag with arms and legs, a sort of giant padded sleep suit that toddlers wear. I was so grateful to her as it enabled me to continue with my studies without my fingers getting too cold to use the laptop.

I was enjoying this opportunity to study with Andrew Womack at the Charis bible college; I was registered for an online course. It was an amazing time of solitude, and as I look back now, it was God’s restorative time for me. I experienced deep peace and felt completely secure and safe, as if I was wrapped in a huge bubble of protection that was almost tangible at times. I grew in knowledge, and faith and wisdom

I was still seeking God daily, asking the question, why was I here? Why here, why now? Just what had God called me to do? It was almost two years since my sabbatical experience, and in that time, I had learned a great deal about the village and my newfound culture and had made friends with many of the villagers. Of course, everyone knew me! I was the white, western woman from England who had come to live on her own in the village. I was quite an anomaly; nobody could quite understand why I would leave my lovely life in the UK to live in a remote village in Moldova.

I was certain that this was where God wanted me to be, but as yet, I hadn't done anything! I had learned the colloquial, which is very important, to understand the culture is crucial, but as yet, I didn't feel that I had achieved anything and was keen to get my teeth into something.

So, I decided to have a time of fasting and praying, seeking God for the what next. After 20 days of fasting and prayer, I was beginning to lose heart. Questioning, did I get it wrong? Maybe I hadn't heard properly, or I needed to do something else to get God's attention. There were many thoughts and frustrations at the time. But just as I was beginning to become disillusioned, Nellie, the Mayor's secretary in the village, visited me.

Nellie asked if I would be willing to look after some of the really desperate elderly people in the village. There were some very frail elderly folk who had absolutely no family to care for them, and Nellie thought that I might be able to help. I could tell she was a little apprehensive asking the question, but my heart was singing as I knew that this ask was coming from God, not from Nellie. This request was my answer to my prayer and fasting, and I was thrilled.

My task was to check in on several elderly folk, to check if they had food, were eating and that they were warm. Maybe do a bit of cleaning for them as they were very frail and basically love and care for them with lots of TLC. I don't think to this day that Nellie had any idea that this was my dream job! As an ex-nurse, I loved to care for people, to provide for their needs and to love them back to wholeness. I was thrilled; I genuinely felt that this was a God appointment and that His heart for me was to serve the elderly and not the youth.

Interesting how we can focus on one area of ministry; I was totally convinced that I was in Moldova for some sort of youth initiative, having worked for seven years with a national youth ministry, Urban Saints (formerly Crusaders), but God had other ideas. My prayers had been answered, and the fasting period rewarded.

I knew that I could really make a difference to the lives of these sad, lonely and impoverished elderly who were desperately in need.

Melia, my first love…

Melia was my first house call; I was a little apprehensive as my language was limited, and I had no idea what to expect. I banged on her door and shouted Buna Ziua, which is Moldovan for good day. After a few minutes, I heard a shuffling and scraping sound coming towards me. I pushed open the door and was greeted by a lady; bent double, pushing a chair, minus a back, along the floor as she was unable to walk unaided. Melia asked, “Cine este?” or Who is it? I told her that the mayor’s office had sent me to help and see how she was doing. At this news, she ushered me to sit down on a small chair beside her bed.

Her room was filthy, and I knew that I would be leaving with a few creatures that I really didn’t want to take home! I had taken a flask of hot sweet tea, which we shared; the tea cut through the cold and warmed us both. There was a small glow from Melia’s soba (log-burning stove), but the room was still cold. As we sat drinking tea and attempting to converse, the hot tea defrosting us both and warming our hearts, we chatted.

Well, at least Melia spoke, and I listened and hardly understood a word as she was speaking Russian! Somehow it didn't seem to matter that I couldn't understand; it was companionship for Melia, a friendly face, someone who could break up her long lonely days. I just prayed that I would nod and smile in all the right places; it seemed to work.

As I sat there drinking the hot tea, me on a chair facing Melia, who was now back in her bed, I noticed that she had many small friends crawling around the room, a mouse running over her table, a rat seemingly warming itself beside the soba. Melia didn't even notice them anymore; I guessed that she must have lived with them for some time. I, on the other hand, had to steel myself to keep smiling and looking at her so as not to run! I knew then that I would be taking a few friends home with me, too, fleas!

I fetched her fresh water from the well and said that I would be back the next day with some hot food and fresh bread; she was absolutely thrilled. We had begun a beautiful journey together; I genuinely loved Melia and taking care of her. We would often sing together. She would sing "Mother of mine" in Russian, and I would sing the "Lord's Prayer" to her in

English. She started to call me “fata mea”, which means my girl. Some of my happiest memories in the village were of sitting in Melia’s rat-infested, flea-ridden home, singing and sharing heart-to-heart a genuine love for one another.

When my language improved, and I began to understand more, I was shocked by the story of Melia’s life. Her story was that of a desperate life of hardship and violence and, in particular, loss. Melia had had a violent husband who beat her and her five children (not an unusual story for this ex-Soviet culture). She was 80 years old when I started caring for her and all her five children were dead! They had all died before the age of 30! Melia’s husband had drunk himself to death.

Melia had lived in her little home all of her life, cooking on the same soba, fetching water from the same well, growing her own vegetables and washing all of her children on the kitchen table, their laundry all scrubbed by hand using water from the well and a tablet of brown soap. The conditions in Moldova remain very harsh, often with Siberian temperatures of -20/30$_{o}$C during the winter. Village life, in particular, is severe. There is still no piped water to the villages and no sanitation, and yet this is Eastern Europe in 2021.

Fortunately, today the towns have begun to change and modernise as more people visit the West and see possibilities. The culture is steadily moving into the 21st century. However, it is not unusual to hear Moldova described as Africa in Europe, especially where village life is concerned.

I was heartbroken when Melia sadly died the following winter. I now had a domiciliary round caring for four senior citizens, three ladies and one man. Anna, Natalia, Lisa, who was completely blind, and Tudor

My task was to visit them two or three times each week; I would take them a hot meal and a flask of hot sweet tea, but more importantly, I would sit on the edge of their beds and just listen to what they had to say. They longed for companionship. With no family, no visitors from the village, and no one to care for them, they were completely isolated.

I drew fresh water from the well, swept their floors, and cleaned their little space as much as they would allow. I made sure that the fire (Soba) was lit to keep them warm, and they were served a hot meal made with love stirred through the middle to give them some real nourishment.

Their little bungalows had just two rooms, but

they lived in one to conserve heat. They all had a Soba, which needed to be lit every day; it had a couple of rings on the top for cooking; it was very primitive but did the job.
Each home had one light switch, one bulb and one plug.
Their furniture was sparse, consisting of a table, a chair and the bed that they were lying on. Every little bungalow was identical; wooden floorboards, and Chalk plaster, white-washed walls. They each had a long drop in the garden for a toilet. The room in which they lived was no more than 6 feet by 9 feet.

I absolutely fell in love with ALL in my care. It was a dream job for me, loving and caring for those desperately in need; I was literally filled with joy every day. I trudged through knee-deep snow with bags of hot food and flasks of sweet tea, sometimes falling as the snow was so deep that I couldn't lift my legs over it. But somehow, I got through; we laughed and cried and sang songs together, and I knew, without doubt, that this was what I had been called to do.

The winter was biting, and the going got really tough; my darlings were getting cold. To keep warm, they would heat water on the Soba and fill a used plastic mineral water bottle (their version of a hot water bottle) which they used to keep themselves warm.

I suggested getting electric blankets from England to keep them warm, but they didn't have a clue what I was talking about, and of course, anything electrical would cost money, and as they only had, at the most, $1 a day as a pension, they were very reluctant to pay for it.

I could only persuade them to try the blankets if I promised to pay their electricity bill. It wasn't a great deal of money for me, but for them, it was a small fortune. So, after some persuasion and a test run of one electric blanket, they were all convinced and enjoying being warm and snug without any financial worries.

We talked about the same things whenever we were chatting over a cup of hot tea, namely, will we have enough wood for the burner? The cost had gone up again, and none of them were sure that they would be able to pay the increase; this was a real concern, especially with the sort of temperatures that we were experiencing.

I appealed to my church for them to have a fund-raising event to raise

supplies of wood for the winter, one supply for each little house to see them through the winter months. They were very happy to do this, always wanting to help and to relieve the suffering and hardships of these villagers.

However, in my prayer time that week I was seeking the Lord for provision for these poor folks when I suddenly had the idea, a God-given light bulb moment, I believe. Why not turn the ground floor of my building into a home for the abandoned elderly? That would mean that in the future, instead of raising funds for four separate houses for fuel etc., we would only need to supply wood for one house where they all lived together in community. A Eureka!! moment.

As soon as I had that thought, a blueprint of the downstairs area was downloaded into my head, and I could see exactly what needed to happen to make this a home for the elderly. Oh, my goodness, my heart was racing; I was so excited and felt sure that this had come directly from above.

I got hold of some graph paper and began drawing plans, just as they had been given to me, for how the ground floor of this derelict building could look. I then had several lengthy conversations with my church Pastor, Tony Summerfield, who agreed to come out to visit the village, to check out what needed to happen and also to experience for himself the plight of these poor souls.

It was arranged for Pastor Tony and his wife, Linda, to fly out to visit me in January 2009. It was the depths of winter when the snow was at its highest level and temperatures were extremely low.

I made a comfortable space for them next to my bedsit on the second floor of the building. I wanted them to have a cosy room that wasn't too cold. I used a plug-in oil-filled radiator to keep the room at a reasonable temperature. They had a small table with a washing-up bowl and 3 inches of hot water lovingly prepared by me each morning to wash in. I had also supplied a torch which would be needed if they wanted to visit the toilet at night. The long drop was at the very back of the garden, one flight of stairs down and some 30 yards or so from the front of the house with no light and an uphill incline. At night it was very precarious. They did have the option of an en-suite facility which, if they chose to use it, consisted of a small bucket with a lid which could be emptied every morning.

I was so glad to welcome Tony and Linda to the village and to enjoy their company, having been there on my own for quite some time. It was lovely to cook for them and to host them as best I could within the limits of the situation.

Pastor Tony and Linda came with me on my rounds one morning and saw the ladies and the conditions in which they lived. We sat with each lady and listened to their tale of woe; they talked and talked and talked. Every visit was well received, and each of the ladies was so utterly delighted to have company and smiling faces. We brought loving, caring hearts into their sad existence for which they were so in need. We prayed for each lady before we left them, and I could tell that my guests were deeply moved by the plight of these amazing elderly folk who were so desperate for help and support and love.

The next day Pastor Tony and I visited the mayor of the village to seek his permission to refurbish the building where I was living into a home for the elderly. He was absolutely thrilled with the concept, and using my hand-drawn plan, he was happy to recruit just the right person who could give a realistic quote for the materials required and also a time scale in which the work could be finished.

Oleg was to be the appointed master builder; he worked with his son Dimitri. We costed the work according to my design, and including labour, the total cost was estimated at 16,000 euros. This was to include a fully fitted kitchen, a shower room, a small room for three single beds and a large room for three beds which also doubled as a sitting room. Each bed in the large room was in a separate cubicle, and each had a pulled curtain for privacy.

My Pastor and his wife returned to the UK, and by the end of May, thanks to every single member of Hitchin Christian Centre (now ZEO church), the funds were raised, and the work began. The miracle of God's Kingdom provision always astounds me! We are so very blessed to be part of God's family, God's economy and on the receiving end of the loving generosity and outpouring of love for His work.

See pictures below.

Oleg fitting electrics

Dimitri digging the cesspit

Sitting room with cubicles

By the end of 2009, Casa Helen was born!

I spent the following three months creating a registered charity in Moldova, which also needed an accountant. The perfect lady was found; Margaretta Brasoveanu had been an accountant for almost 30 years. Margaretta worked for all the local grocery stores in many villages across the region and had a fabulous reputation. The best thing was that Margaretta lived in the village and her house was next door to Casa Helen. We still have Margaretta now, and she has proved invaluable over the years.

I recruited a manager, Dina Ciaburu, a beautiful Christian lady who had made my stay in the village so easy through her warm heart and hospitality, always looking after me and baking delicious meals. I also hired a cook, a couple of carers and a man to stoke the boiler to keep us all warm. I continued to live on the premises in my little bedsit upstairs, and we soon became one big family.

We moved the ladies in March 2010, but sadly, Tudor didn't want to come. I suspect that as the lone male, he was a little intimidated. The concept of community living in a care home was very new to the culture, and even the ladies had to be persuaded that it was a good thing. Once they had moved in, however, they totally saw the benefits, and it became a very happy home.

Ana, Dina, Me and Natalia

Lisa the blind lady, Ana and Natalia 2010

Margarette with her husband Nicolae

A more recent photo

We have now expanded and can provide beds for 22 ladies.

Casa Helen is a very happy place, filled with love and care. We have the best carers, totally dedicated to the ladies. Our cook provides delicious meals three times a day, and we host many celebrations.

It wasn't always plain sailing; we had much opposition, initially from some of the people in the village who told me constantly that it wouldn't work. It was a concept that they didn't understand, and they told me in no uncertain terms that the elderly people would not come!

However, they did come, and they now enjoy living in a community where all their needs are provided for, where they can live as one big family, loving and supporting one another and providing the companionship that was so missing when the ladies lived in complete isolation.

Casa Helen has and always will have my heart; it was birthed from a God-given vision. We had our challenges, but I realised early on that it was God's will, and when that is the case, nothing can stop progress. It may have taken longer than I wanted, but we had the best people on board, and now the village is very proud of the fact that they have a home for the elderly. This gives them status as there are less than a handful of such residencies in Moldova.

Casa Helen is a miracle. A God-given vision that was provided for entirely by the selfless generosity of Hitchin Christian Centre congregation. And from concept to finished building, it was just one year. There were so many obstacles along the way and despite the opposition from the villagers, we kept going forward and pushed through.

Casa Helen is a beautiful place, and all who visit are moved by the atmosphere. There is no doubt in my mind that this is no less than a house of God; Casa Helen has His heart.

You may be wondering why the name Casa Helen, so let me explain. The building was initially purchased by a young family in HCC who had been left a sum of money in their aunt's will. They decided to tithe the money, which was the exact sum we required to purchase the building. That aunt was called Helen Mary Smith, and Helen had expressed that something good should come from her gift. The family decided that this was a great use of the tithe; we wanted to honour Helen Mary Smith, so we called the home Casa Helen.

The lady that nobody wanted

We received a call at Casa Helen from a young man in Chisinau, Moldova's capital city. Chisinau, at that time, was almost 3 hours drive from our little village. We were curious to know how the caller had heard about Casa Helen as we had never advertised.

The caller asked if we had a bed for a lady in her late 50s, and he said that he could pay 100 euros a month for her care which was far more than we would normally ask for a month's care and accommodation.

We asked the usual questions regarding mobility as we really didn't have the facilities or number of carers required to assist with patients who were unable to walk. It was important, therefore, to know whether the person was able to get to the toilet and to the dining room with minimal assistance.

The young man assured us that the lady (who he said was his aunt) could walk and would have no difficulties in this area. We agreed that he would accompany her the next day to Casa Helen, and they would be taking the bus and then a taxi from the bus station.

We prepared her bed and awaited her arrival. When Irina (the aunt) arrived at Casa Helen, we saw immediately that she had bandages on both legs, was unable to speak and was in a poor state of alertness. We were shocked at her condition and felt that we needed to get her into a bed as soon as possible so that we could assess her.

It took three people to get her to her bed as she was too weak to move. The young man dropped her bag of medication at our feet, threw 100 euros on the bed and ran, saying he'd be back in a month to see how she was. Needless to say, we never saw him again.

We bathed her, put her in a clean nightie, and dressed her legs which were completely black and necrosed with gangrene. We also discovered a bed sore on her back, a hole in her flesh the size of a man's fist.

Her eyes were open but empty; she seemed to be far away. Her wounds were so bad and so deep that there was no more pain or sensation, just the stench of rotting flesh.

Anna, one of our carers, felt called to look after this lady and became her main carer, feeding her a little soup each day and taking care of all of her needs.

We were all devastated to read the medical notes that accompanied Irina. They told us that she had syphilis, that she was an alcoholic, that she had been abused sexually and physically for most of her life, and that her limbs had become rotten through extreme cold conditions and neglect.

For three months, Anna cared for her almost every day, showing her loving care and keeping her clean and comfortable and at peace. I believe this was the first time in her life that this poor lady was shown any love, compassion, or care.

I was hosting a National Women's Conference a few weeks later and had invited a couple of Christian leaders, Margaret Stunt and Rachel Hickson, to Casa Helen to pray for Irina, who was rapidly deteriorating. We stood around her bed with Anna, her main carer and prayed her into the arms of Jesus. I firmly believed that

He wanted her to be loved and cared for at Casa Helen for the final months of her life, to be prayed for, loved and shown compassion.

The following morning, we were shocked to hear that Anna, Irina's carer, had died in her sleep (at 56 years old!). This was totally unexpected as she was sprightly and hard-working and seemed so young at heart. We were all in shock!

Irina also left us a few hours later, which was expected. I have often mulled over the events of that last day. Prayer warriors, Pastors, Anna and I praying for Irina and then they are both within hours taken to be with the Lord.

I spent some time talking to Jesus about this and wondering why

Anna had to go too and first. I had a real sense that Jesus had taken her to welcome Irina home, as I don't believe there would have been anyone she knew in heaven to greet her.

I know this is my interpretation, and there is no actual biblical basis for my conclusions. However, I know my Jesus, and He would be filled with compassion and love for Irina and for Anna, who dedicated herself to serving Irina in her last months.

Anna would be standing ready to embrace Irina in her new complete, and beautiful body and would be able to experience perfect peace and joy for the first time in her life. Miraculously, through the love of Jesus.

Chapter 5

Our Very Own Well

Whilst taking a short break in the UK one time, I was privileged to be invited to have lunch with the amazing Rachel Hickson, Founder of "Heartcry for Change", which is a ministry based in Oxford. Rachel had become a very dear friend, a constant encourager and a most welcome mentor to me—all of those wonderful attributes were extremely valuable to me whilst serving in Moldova.

During lunch, Rachel asked me what was the most pressing need for Casa Helen. I didn't need to think for a nanosecond as I knew exactly what we needed… Our own source of drinking water.

We laughed as I recounted the numerous times I had visited the well down the hill and was unable to stand up due to the extreme icy conditions. It was almost impossible to draw water without ending up flat on my back. Then the challenge of carrying two buckets of water uphill in knee-deep snow and ice! Our nearest well was down the hill, three hundred metres away, next to the village school.

The winters were bleak, and the little metal bucket and chain which reached into the abyss of the well was often frozen solid to the concrete rim of the well mouth. Often whilst chipping off the ice, my feet would slip on the frozen lake of spilt water under my feet. Inevitably, invariably, I would end up flat on my back, unable to stand!

Here is the well I regularly visited to draw water.

It was fun to recount some of the hairier moments visiting the well down the lane, trying to stay upright on thick ice whilst trying to carry a bucket of water!!! Rachel and I laughed together as I shared some of the funnier episodes. Lunch was great, and Rachel, as ever full of encouragement and praise. I always left her feeling invincible, that I really could conquer the world for Jesus whilst helping others to feel valued and special. The way that Rachel made me feel.

As we said our goodbyes that day, Rachel pressed something into my hand and said that she hoped it would cover the costs of a well which could be installed in our garden at Casa Helen. Imagine my delight when I uncurled my fingers to discover a cheque for $2000!! Eureka! My prayers had been answered; thank you, Rachel.

And so, the miracle began to unfold…My first challenge was to find a person who could, indeed, dig a well. I had absolutely no experience whatsoever and wasn't sure even where we should begin to dig. I asked one of the locals to help me to identify the spot where the well should be.

Everyone told me to call the diviner, who would use his sticks to find water beneath the ground. Feeling very unsure about this, I decided to spend some time with the Lord. I knew the Old Testament said not to use divination, and so I was very uneasy to go down that route.

I took myself off for a day's prayer and dreaming with the Lord. I drew an outline of the garden at Casa Helen, and I placed a cross in each of the areas that would have enough space for a Well to be installed.

I prayed and asked God just where it should be. I divided my drawing into four individual parts and folded each piece of paper into very tiny squares. There were four pieces of paper representing the four quarters of the garden and four crosses marking the possible locations for a well. I placed these pieces of paper on my open bible and prayed, "Where, Lord?"

I then closed my eyes and told God that the piece of paper I chose with my eyes closed, I would believe that He had chosen, not me, as the exact location of the new well. I took a deep breath, eyes tight shut and felt around for one of the folded pieces of paper and picked one.

Excited to see the result, I opened my eyes and unfolded the paper. So, all was revealed, the well would be dug on the left side of the garden, just past the gate and in front of the kitchen.

I was so sure that this was exactly the right place and that God had chosen it, not me. My next move was to find the man who had the huge drilling equipment to drill down around 15 metres.

It was quite an operation. An everyday occurrence for the expert driller who did this sort of thing ALL the time. But, for me, it was absolutely fascinating to see just how it happened.

My neighbours had been to visit to tell me not to dig where God had told me to dig. Some of the villagers said I was foolish to even try as I wouldn't find water and that "I was wasting my time and money". Some told me they had a well 30 metres deep, and it was empty! So, amid the negativity and criticism and discouragement, I trusted and proceeded.

I was sure that God had provided, that He had chosen the spot and that we would definitely find water! My experience is always that if God gives the provision and resources, then the project is secure and successful. Even in the midst of opposition and, nay sayers!

The day finally arrived when the digging would commence. First, the men came with their large shovels; we had seven in total. Their job was to clear the earth as the drill, which was one metre in diameter, sunk deep down into the earth to find water.

Then, the earth began to shake, and we could no longer hear ourselves speak as the ginormous drill rounded the hill, arriving at the front of the house. Behind the drill, a heavy goods vehicle was carrying 15-metre-deep concrete rings to form the walls of the well.

All the village came to watch the spectacle. All the critics and sceptics came out in force, smiling and shaking their heads. The work began at 8.00 am. Mounds of soil and gravel were shovelled into the back of a lorry as the drill sunk deeper and deeper into the earth. It was an incredibly exciting sight for me, a complete novice; never had I seen anything like this.

Just after 11.00 am, after watching for what seemed like an eternity, we decided to make a brew and provide refreshments and well-earned sandwiches for the workers.

We had just begun preparing the food when the owner of the digger raced up the garden path to the kitchen, shouting, "We have water, we have water!" What a joyous moment that was! We all gasped in amazement. They were only down 10 metres, and already water was springing from the earth. The locals were shocked; they couldn't believe it. I praised the Lord and thanked Him for his faithfulness.

The men proceeded to lower the concrete rings into the hole, 10 in total, and then they placed one decorative ring on top with a mock "Jack and Jill" looking roof to form the decorative top of the well, which was bright red.

Of course, the well needed to settle, and the water needed to be sent away for analysis before we could use it. But we had done it. We had water, and, in a few weeks, we would be able to use it, provided the analysis was favourable.

Just one month later, following testing, we were informed that the water was the purest that they had found in the village and that we had hit a natural spring that was running underground. How incredible was that? A true miracle of God given provision, His direction and faithfulness.

We invited all the villagers to come and drink deeply from the well. To use it for their needs as well as ours. A God provision that would provide for all who were thirsty. The well is for everyone, and because it is close to the front gate, it is easy to access

This same well still provides the purest water for all who wish to draw from it.

Here is the actual well at Casa Helen and one of our precious grannies, drawing water

Jesus answered, “If you drink from Jacob’s well, you’ll be thirsty again, [14] but if anyone drinks the living water I give them, they will never be thirsty again. For when you drink the water I give you, it becomes a gushing fountain *of the Holy Spirit*, flooding you with endless life!” John 4:13

Chapter 6

Time for a Break! Or was it?

I was feeling very tired, having lived and worked in Moldova full-time since 2007, so I decided to come home for a break. I was in need of R&R and some serious prayer ministry. I was feeling that my time in the village had come to a close, and it was time to move on and settle again in the UK. However, I had nowhere to live, and my only financial support was from my church, so I applied to Hitchin town council for a flat. I was told, sadly, that I wasn't eligible and would have to be homeless for six months to qualify.

God had other plans. A young couple from my church contacted me to say that they were going to Taiwan to live and needed someone to house-sit their property in the UK. Would I like to live in their little cottage? I was absolutely thrilled. It was right in the centre of Hitchin town so no transport was required. I could take the bus, walk to town and to my church and shop at a local supermarket close by. It was absolutely perfect.

31 Each and every day He will supply your needs as you seek His kingdom passionately, above all else. 32 So don't ever be afraid, dearest friends! Your loving Father joyously gives you His kingdom realm with all its promises! Luke 12:31.32

I felt it was time for a rest. The mission field can be exhausting; living and working in a different language and culture is extremely tiring at times. I had pioneered something of a novelty in Casa Helen, as homes for the elderly were a very new concept. It had been an extremely challenging few years. I had a great deal of opposition, trying to establish a very novel concept that everyone thought would fail!

I was now thinking I would return to my life in England and visit the project 3-4 times a year. So, I came home for a break and, to my surprise, was invited to work for Mission Direct two days a week as their fundraising director. I loved my job; I was living rent-free in my God-given cottage, earning just enough to get by, I had a little pussy cat called Fred who was such a joyous companion, and I could see my grandchildren every day.

I was very happy in Hitchin, reconnecting full-time with my church family and also with my children, who were all in or close to Hitchin. I began to feel very settled and happy and was even able to organise women's conferences in Moldova from England.

I visited the country several times in the year and found that through email and Skype, it wasn't difficult to work in Moldova from the UK. I checked in with Casa Helen regularly, invited speakers from around the world to teach and preach at our ladies' conferences, and everything seemed to be working well.

However, God had other ideas about me staying in the UK. He began to speak to me about a very different project. This is how it happened…

I had connected a little with a wonderful missionary couple from Denmark who were working with disadvantaged girls, mentoring and training them in life skills. Teaching them about Jesus and developing them into leaders in the church.

I learned that 400,000 girls were missing from Moldova at the hands of human traffickers who were forcing them into prostitution and shipping them to other countries like Turkey, Germany, and Holland, to name but a few. I became passionate about the cause.

It was October 2012 when I was visiting Moldova to attend a women's conference that I and a team from Moldova had organised.

The conference was to be held in Chisinau, the capital city, and we had invited some amazing women speakers from the UK,

Australia and Canada. Tickets had been snapped up, and we had around 1,000 women registered!

The ladies in Moldova were extremely poor in spirit and of very low self-worth. Many were now single parents, trying to raise children on very little income and their husbands had either found work in another country or had left, never to return again. Moldova was and still is a very male-dominated culture, and women were permanently oppressed and of little worth in the eyes of men.

However, God wanted them to know what His opinion was of them. Through the church and our conferences, He began to instil self-worth in His girls, to provide opportunities for leadership and to grow women of stature and influence. Much fruit was generated as women took up the invitation to be prayed for and to receive Jesus into their lives. They came in their hundreds, running to the front of the conference hall, giving their lives to the Lord Jesus!

Margaret Stunt was invited as our key speaker and travelled from Australia to be with us. Margaret was a precious friend of mine who had mentored and steered my faith journey for many years. Her message for the women of Moldova was transformational, and many lives were changed. (These conferences are now an annual event beginning in the UK and then travelling to Moldova).

Whilst we were attending the conference, Margaret and I were lodged in a gypsy caravan loaned to us by the Danish mission couple, Charlotte and Johannes. We lived in a very confined space for four days and used this time for prayer, dreaming, visioning and sharing what God was saying to us at that time.

This was to be caravan experience number 1.

We were talking and dreaming together one day, and it was then that I felt the first nudge from the Lord, telling me that this caravan was going to be my new home. I experienced a deep sense of peace and felt that this little home was just such a beautiful place to be. I was to establish a safe home for young girls who were at risk of being trafficked and betrayed into prostitution. I was convinced that God had spoken that day and filled me with passion for the plight of these girls.

A few weeks passed, and now back in the UK, I began to think that I hadn't heard from the Lord. Had I imagined this experience? Did I really hear from God, or was I just dreaming and scheming? However, that same day I had a telephone call from a wonderful lady in

Herefordshire who had been a very definite part of my journey, Jill Lawson.

Jill offered me her caravan, which was positioned, just over the border of Herefordshire into Wales. I decided to take some time out there for a holiday and some respite and took her up on her generous offer.

This was to be caravan experience number 2.

So now we are two caravans in; there seems to be something going on with caravans. Whilst enjoying this retreat in Jill's caravan in Wales, I picked up a book on her shelf called "Journey into God's Heart" by Jennifer Reece Larkham. It was an incredible read and told of Jennifer's journey through divorce after 30 years of marriage, a journey very similar to mine.

I so related to Jennifer that I decided to email her ministry, "Beauty from Ashes", and make an appointment to see her. I also discovered that she was a good friend of Jill Lawson, who was mentioned in her book and in whose caravan, I was resting.

Between my stay in the second caravan and meeting Jen was about six weeks. I was praying and asking God for the "what next" and questioning, "Do you REALLY want me to go back to Moldova?" Had I heard him properly? I had become rather settled in Hitchin, and everything was working well, both at home and in Moldova, so the thought of returning to live there was not thrilling me at this stage!

My appointment time had arrived, and I travelled to the house where Jennifer lives in Tonbridge and was shown into the hall. This beautiful petite lady with a beaming smile came to meet me and informed me that there was no room at the inn. All the prayer rooms were occupied that day, so she would have to find somewhere else for us to talk and pray. Jen assured me that she had just the right place at the bottom of the garden for us to talk and pray in private.

I really do think God has a sense of humour. When we reached the bottom of her spacious garden, Jen opened the door of the oldest battered caravan I had ever seen and ushered me in. I laughed as I knew the minute, we walked into it that this was my sign to go back to Moldova.

Caravan experience number 3!

I needed to pick up where I had left off and live in the caravan where I had originally dreamed the dream of helping those unfortunate girls. God speaks in many ways, and somehow you just know, as He joins the dots, there is no way out; we must go.

"The ultimate measure of a man/woman is not where he/she stands in moments of comfort and convenience, but where he/she stands at times of challenge and controversy." ~ Martin Luther King, Jr.

How was I to go this time? I shared my dream with my church and with my prayer group. An amazing group of people who met regularly to pray for me and the work in Moldova and had been so faithful, not just in prayer but also in practical and financial support and encouragement. I loved them dearly.

I felt that I needed transport and that the best vehicle would be a sturdy jeep as the roads in Moldova were mud tracks most of the time and full of potholes. I wasn't bothered about the age of the jeep just as long as it had a reputation for reliability, strength, and please let it be red, Salvation colours! I had been praying this very specific prayer for many months.

I travelled to various churches during the next few months, talking about my experience in Moldova and also the plight of girls at risk from traffickers. I shared my vision of providing a shelter for girls to keep them safe. Where we would be able to educate, nurture and teach life skills that would help those at risk in their future development. Many were village girls who had not had a good education and were easy prey for men who would take advantage of their innocence.

The churches listened and supported me and were extremely encouraging, some even continuing with me on the journey and becoming long-term partners. "Heartcry for Change", an amazing ministry led by Rachel Hickson and Helen Azer, had also pledged support for the long term and introduced me to Gill and Paul Trevor.

Gill was on the board of trustees for "Heartcry for Change", and they had discussed the vision of the shelter for at-risk girls and how they could best support us.

Gill and Paul then invited me to speak at their church near Wolverhampton. Following the service, they totally overwhelmed me by presenting me with a jeep, not just any jeep but something really sturdy, a Mitsubishi Shogun. It was absolutely perfect for my needs and also, would you believe it… deep red!

Whoop! God had answered my very specific prayer with a very specific response.

We worship the God who can do immeasurably more than we could ever hope or dream for!! Ephesians 3:20

I now know for sure that God was in every move I made, and He was providing for every step of my return journey.

I had been working for Mission Direct as their fundraising director for 18 months and really enjoyed my time there. I love working with the amazing team of people, and so it was all a little sad to be parting ways so soon. On my last Friday, they arranged a beautiful tea for me and asked me to share my plans with them for my return to Moldova.

I was very excited now about returning but was struggling to raise the funds that were necessary to be able to drive the jeep to Moldova over a period of four days; this included a three night stay, and I needed enough money to fill the fuel tank four or five times as it was a 1600-mile trip. The estimated sum that I needed was £600.

That same morning, I had been asking God for His provision for my trip and asking why I wasn't in the best position; after all, I had given away everything and wasn't at all materialistic. I was travelling with the bare minimum.

God's response was immediate; He said, "You only gave what you didn't want!" In other words, it hadn't really cost me anything emotionally or otherwise.

So, I decided to ask Him what it was that He wanted me to give away. WARNING don't ask this sort of question if you are not prepared to do whatever God wants you to do!

To my utter surprise, a picture of my very, very favourite coat popped into my head! It was my prize possession; a Jasper Conran swing mac in navy with white polka dots, and I absolutely loved it.

NOOOOOOO was the cry that came out of me; you cannot be serious!" But He was, and I found myself on my last day at Mission Direct taking my favourite coat into work to give to a young woman God had shown me.

You see, sometimes there can be a blockage, and we need to clear it for God provision to flow again. He loves to test the depth of our love for Him.

So, here's the miracle…

After our tea and my sharing about the journey on which I was about to embark, Jackie, a senior member of the team, said that they had collected from all the staff and wanted me to receive a gift.

She was holding a small manila envelope with my name on it. Jackie asked me how I would feel if it was a cheque for £100, and I responded with a thank you, that would be absolutely fantastic. Then she asked how would it feel if they were to give me £300? I am now grinning from ear to ear at the possibility of having half the funds needed for my trip. (None of the team knew anything of my conversation with Jesus that morning!)

Then Jackie said what if the contents of this envelope were a cheque for £600? How incredible was that! The tears of joy began to flow, and I knew that out of their generous hearts, they had answered God's prompting to supply my immediate needs, and all it had cost me was my favourite Jasper Conran coat!

I will never forget their generosity to me; they released an avalanche of cash gifts that I was about to receive once my feet touched the soil of Moldova. I was on my way…

Chapter 7

God - The Dream Catcher!

When I first met Marie, she was 11 years old. A very beautiful gypsy girl from an extremely dysfunctional family. Her mother, who had given birth to her at a very young age, was about to sell her to traders for her to be sexually exploited. When Charlotte, our Danish missionary leader, heard what was rumoured across our small town, she acted quickly and found space in one of our caravans for her to be kept safe, warm, fed and very much protected from those who would sell her on.

Charlotte spoke to her mother and said that she would supply a box of food every week to help the family on condition that she agreed to release Marie into our care at the mission. Her mother agreed, thankfully, and Marie, who had been sleeping in a broken "Silver Cross" style baby pram, now found herself in a warm, loving environment and in a proper bed.

When we asked her why she chose to sleep in the pram instead of on the floor with the rest of her family, she told us that when sleeping on the ground, the little creatures would come and nibble her face. The family was riddled with rats and mice, and Marie had the scars to show where her face had been bitten in the night by rats!

Charlotte, who was studying to be a children's social worker, quickly met with the authorities with whom she had built very good relationships. Many had been on the receiving end of second-hand clothing, which our mission had distributed from Denmark. Also, the Social Services department had often called on Charlotte and Johannes to clothe and equip families who literally had nothing, knowing that they regularly received HGV's full of good quality humanitarian aid from Denmark and the Faro Islands.

The social work department helped us to secure an official court order to protect Marie and to prove that we had legally taken her in from a dangerous situation. The plan was to teach her to read and write and to do basic math before approaching the school to ask if she could attend. Many gypsy children were denied access to school as they were often without shoes, or clean clothing, and they were considered extremely unhygienic and to be avoided.

Marie came to us with hair full of lice and clothing full of fleas, so there was work to be done to make sure that she was accepted into society. We could see that she was a very clever girl and was eager to learn. Marie was washed, polished, deloused and dressed beautifully. She has hair that is thick, black and curly and needed a really good cut.

One day we tried at least six hair salons before we could find someone willing to cut her hair. The culture was so riddled with prejudice, especially toward gypsy families.

Meanwhile, Marie, who had never had such lovely clean clothes, regular food, and a warm bed to sleep in, was extremely happy. Her mum would come to the mission sometimes to have breakfast with us. Marie would join us and chat with her mum, which kept the relationship without putting Marie in danger. It was very clear that she wanted to stay in the mission; she enjoyed her lessons and never wanted to go back to the family.

Charlotte had established a small classroom for disadvantaged children, some from gypsy families (that were not allowed to go to a mainstream school), some children were from alcoholic parents who were unable to care for them, and some children who had special educational and physical needs. Marie came to school every day and gradually began to learn her numbers and how to read. She learned basic arithmetic, how to write, and was fed on story books and, of course, the bible stories.

Charlotte kept her promise and helped her family a great deal with new clothing, mattresses and bedding, food parcels etc., and they seemed very content with that.

One Christmas time, we had given Marie's family a huge hamper with everything they would possibly need for a glorious Christmas feast. That same day her mum was seen begging by the local market in the snow, sitting on a piece of cardboard on the ground.

Vanya, one of our team, went to speak to her and asked, "What are you doing? We gave you a hamper and gifts for Christmas; why do you sit here in the freezing winter, begging?" Marie's mum replied, "I'm hoping to get enough money for a bottle of champagne to go with the food!" When Vanya told us of her response, we laughed and laughed. What else could we do!?

Marie was the first of many young girls who we began to identify as particularly vulnerable; we worked more closely with Social Services and began to accompany the team from the Social Care office to visit families in the villages. We could see for ourselves the great need for education of young girls, some who were already being used as the village prostitute because they didn't know any different!

We took in another girl whose father had died of a drug overdose and whose mother was working in Moscow and only came home for two weeks in the summer. Victoria was living with her granny, who didn't seem to like her very much. The relationship was broken; however, Victoria seemed like a very nice girl. She was 13 when a policeman brought her to the mission; he had found her in a sauna complex where men would regularly go for sex with young girls.

The story was that Victoria had tried to run away from her grandma and had been picked up by men in a car who were on their way to the sauna. Fortunately, the police had raided the sauna complex that day, found Victoria and realising that she was just 13, they brought her to Charlotte.

The Mission was beginning to be recognised as a safe place for young girls at risk from traffickers and others locally who would violate and degrade young girls for sexual pleasure.

The work with the girls grew very quickly, and the space in the caravans just wasn't enough; we needed a small house which would house many more girls. Johannes, who had been making enquiries and looking for properties, had found a small bungalow that had the potential to be converted into a lovely home for girls. Charlotte and I decided to visit the property to have a look around, to pray and to discern whether this was the one.

We prayed for a sign that this property was God's choice; we prayed very specifically that we would find a bible somewhere on the premises. There was not one scrap of furniture, only piles of rubbish, so the prospects of finding a bible in this place were very slim indeed. As we looked around, in one corner of a room, there was a large, battered and extremely dirty cardboard box filled with old bottles, rags, torn papers and much dirt.

We started to lift things out of the box to see if there was anything of worth in it, and…, yes, you guessed it! To our surprise, we found an old, very dusty bible.

However, that wasn't enough confirmation for Charlotte, so she asked God for a second sign. This time as we searched amongst the debris in the box, we found an empty liqueur bottle; it had held cherry liqueur. It wasn't a random cherry liqueur but a very special liqueur, a product of Denmark!

The chances of finding a Danish product in Moldova was extremely rare. Again, Charlotte said, let's ask for one more confirmation. We committed the classic, no, no, picked up the bible, opened it at a random page, Charlotte prayed and with her eyes closed, then put her finger on a verse. There we read, "The earth is the Lords and everything in it!"

That was it, all that we needed; we felt that God was confirming our request, answering our every prayer and that He was saying, this property is mine, and I am giving it to you!

However, we still needed to find the money even though we felt sure we were in the right place. A few weeks later, a wonderful couple from England, Gill and Paul Trevor, mentioned in the earlier chapters, came to visit.

We were keen to update them on the progress of the rescue operation of the village girls and to show them our potential new shelter, which would need a considerable amount of work to make it habitable. Paul asked how much we were looking for to purchase the bungalow. We needed 4,000 Euros, a small sum compared to house prices in the UK. We had been gifted part of the total cost, but the 4,000 remained outstanding, and we had no way of paying it. As soon as we shared the outstanding amount with Paul, he said, it's yours!

How fantastic, there was a great deal of rejoicing that day, praising God for His goodness. Paul and Gill were on the board of Heartcry for Change and had been sent with their blessing to offer just what we needed for refurbishing the bungalow and making it into a beautiful little shelter for the girls.

Johannes recruited a team to work with him, and it seemed just a matter of a few weeks until completion. It is now a beautiful, refurbished space which can house 12 girls together with their live-in carers; we refer to it as the Shelter, a place of new beginnings.

The girls who live in the shelter were 11yrs to 16yrs old and attended the local school in town as we wanted them to have a good foundational education. Life skills and mentoring were conducted after school, and the girls were taught personal hygiene, food preparation, how to keep house, how to speak politely in social circles, and basic etiquette. They attended church every Sunday and learned about Jesus.

The girls met with Jesus, and many have accepted Him into their lives and are passionate followers of Him. His presence brings them to a place of complete healing, emotionally and physically. They are able to exercise forgiveness for those who have abused them, in particular, their parents.

It soon became clear that we needed a phase two, a residential centre which could house girls of 16+ and prepare them for a future that would enable them to become independent and self-sufficient as none of the girls had parents to encourage or provide for them financially.

We began dreaming and praying and planning for phase two, for an educational training/vocational centre for the girls where they could experience further education, learn business skills, business planning, accounting, and website design. We wanted to encourage them to fulfil their dreams and release their entrepreneurial gifts.

Our little church met in one corner of a very large and ugly Soviet-style building. The floor which we inhabited was cold and dank, and dilapidated. We needed a massive refurbishment. But we never had the finances to develop the church/educational/community space we dreamed of. The church owned a very small corner of the third floor of the building; the remaining floor area was completely derelict. We needed to purchase the whole of the floor if we were to establish a fully equipped residential, educational centre and a church community space.

We had plans which included: -

- A new space for the church, new windows, and a kitchen to feed those in need.
- A shower and toilet block so that people can find hot running water, clean

clothing, finding hope and dignity from poverty and despair.

- A Youth room with a kitchen, games room and toilets etc
- A residential academy that would have four dormitories, a fitted kitchen, a lounge space, bathrooms and toilets and a separate mini apartment for live-in house parents.

As we were considering the cost of all that needed to happen, I was surprised to receive an invitation to attend a party which was to be held at a church in Vienna. The Senior Pastor, Angela Gaiter, was celebrating her birthday. Angela was, at that time, unknown to me but was a very good friend of Rachel Hickson.

Angela and Gianni, her Italian husband, had spent 20 years planting many churches across Vienna, and that had been their sole focus. Suddenly, God was speaking to her about connecting with a mission team in another country, and Rachel told her about our work in Moldova.

So, I left my little caravan for a few days, took an all-expenses paid trip to Vienna and spent a wonderful evening at Angela's birthday party, getting to know her and talking about all that was happening in Moldova.

I told her about Casa Helen, about my heart for women to release them into God-given potential, about our conferences and about our recent endeavours, rescuing vulnerable girls from the villages in Moldova. Preventing them from being stolen, abused and/or trafficked.

I enjoyed a fantastic experience of church in Vienna and felt privileged to be invited to share about the mission and team in Moldova, which I was representing. It was a truly blessed time.

I travelled back to my little caravan a few days later and shared all that had happened during the party; I had met so many wonderful people, had been interviewed on stage and felt quite the celebrity. Also, I had eaten some incredible Viennese food, enjoyed some amazing hospitality and had a really super time.

The following week, I received an email from Angela and to my amazement, she stated that she had received, in total, 14,000 Euros in birthday gifts. Her next line blew me away… I would like it to be used for the rescuing and education of vulnerable girls. How incredible was that?

It occurred to me that whilst I wasn't sure about my return to Moldova and was indeed hesitant, my obedience had paid off.

Had I not answered the call, I would not have had an opportunity to connect with Angela, and the large gift of 14,000 Euros would not have materialised. Through obedience to the call, God had begun to pour out His blessings, and He never stopped; however, please read on, for the best bit is yet to come…

Johannes, meanwhile, was meeting with the owners of the building to determine how much we would need to invest in order to own the whole of the third floor. It was an enormous space and would take a great deal of refurbishment to realise our dream, but we felt the first step was to purchase the entire space.

We were all amazed when the answer was 14,000 Euros! Praise the Lord; He had done it again!

And so it began; the full floor area was purchased, and we began to pray and seek God for His help and His resourcing. Money began to trickle in slowly and steadily, the space began to take shape.

We decided to make the space for the girls a priority, together with installing a heating system that would service the whole floor.

By 2021 The girl's residential Academy was now complete, and last year, they launched a diploma in business studies which was to be completed over twelve months. Both residential and non-residential students attended over 16 years of age. On completion, if successful, they will be awarded a diploma in business skills.

Three of the girls who completed the business skills course.

The church and kitchen facilities at the opposite end of the floor space are well on the way to completion.

The project began small, ten years ago, which may seem a long time for some. However, it does take time, and there were many unforeseen incidences that we didn't expect along the way.

The work goes on, and it is thrilling to see these girls living faith-filled lives, full of Jesus, healed and whole! Whilst I no longer live in Moldova, our foundation, Love Moldova, remains very active, providing financial support, prayer and encouragement to all.

Our amazing God has provided and continues to provide for our every need. The centre has rescued and educated more than 22 girls so far, and there are many more who need our help.

We have conducted educational seminars in schools and in local villagers to raise awareness of the risk of being trafficked. We have highlighted the dangers of believing the lies of those who would entice girls into a life of misery in the sex trade. Many, sadly, are never seen again. It is often a family member trying to dupe the young girl knowing that he (sometimes she) can earn considerable money from this elicit cargo. The problem remains, but awareness is crucial, and we will continue our campaign to educate the world regarding the evil traffickers who steal young people. They use young girls, in particular, for sexual pleasure, generating millions of pounds for the perpetrators.

There are currently 400,000 girls missing from Moldova, duped or snatched by the hands of traffickers! Moldova is the size of Wales, and the figure of 400,000 equates to the whole of Cardiff's population suddenly disappearing!

If you would like to learn more about this despicable trade, the link below will take you to a documentary; interviewing girls who have been rescued from the hands of traffickers. The movie is set in Moldova, which is referred to as the trafficking engine of the world! https://www.youtube.com/watch?v=MFaDHgXPbUg

If you would like to experience Moldovan culture for yourself, it is available through our website: - www.lovemoldova.foundation

Chapter 8

Women: God's Secret Weapon

"The devil knows that when women find out who they really are and how they play a significant role in the downfall of his kingdom, his kingdom will come to an abrupt end...Women have not been relegated to posts as mere privates in God's army; indeed, they have been chosen as key players. The biblical record shows that, from Rahab to Mary to Pricilla, God has used women to transform cities, regions and the world."- Ed Silvoso

One of the main highlights of my time in Moldova was organising the annual women's conference at the Leo Grand Hotel in Chisinau, the capital city. We held four conferences consecutively, from a pilot conference in Balti to staging three further conferences in the city between 2009 and 2012.

I have a huge heart and passion to see women released into their full potential. To place on each woman's heart their true value and to encourage them on their journey to total fulfilment in Jesus.

If you are indeed a woman reading this, let me ask the question of you…

Do you know your worth? Your true value? Your potential? Have you found your "sweet spot"? That place which brings you alive. The moment when we realise that THIS (whatever THIS is) is what we were born for, our role in this life becomes sweet and full of joyful fulfilment! This is our destiny, our God-Given Purpose!

Many years ago, I studied "Strength Finder," a personality profiling that discovered your top 30 strengths but focused on the top 5. The whole journey was a tremendous revelation to me and affirmed that the role I was currently employed to do, was absolutely perfect for me.

No wonder I had such enjoyment going to work every day; it was always a joy! I learned that if we are **not** doing what we were created to do, the thing that brings us the most joy and fulfilment, at least 70% of the day, then we are in the wrong place. A square peg in a round hole, a very poor fit.

Background

During my life in Moldova, I learned how life must have been for the people during Soviet Communist rule. They were never able to find their true identities; they certainly wouldn't have been afforded the privilege of finding out just what their key strengths were. Neither would they be able to choose in which line of employment they would like to outwork those gifts. Gifts that would allow them to be able to live a full and rewarding life. Quite the contrary, following the second world war, the people had no rights; no encouragement or inclination to dream because the system was such that everyone was treated as robots.

All entrepreneurial visionaries and educated people were suppressed or removed. They were either shot or sent to Siberia to work in the labour camps. All the God-given dreams and giftings that had been put inside of them were stifled and suffocated due to the regime!

To even hope for something better was impossible; thus was the system, and ALL had to conform.

"We don't let them have ideas. Why would we let them have guns?"
— Joseph Stalin

People were told what to do, and everyone was part of a working cooperative which was government owned. All wages were the same; all children were raised in state kindergartens so that their parents could work in the cooperative, usually working the land for long hours.

A quote from the people of that time "**We will pretend to work, and they will pretend to pay us.**"

"Where there is no vision, the people perish" Proverbs 29:18

The people at that time became robotic, stagnating mentally, not encouraged to think, dream or even to consider an alternative way of life. Their only choice was to conform.

"Education is a weapon whose effect depends on who holds it in his hands and at whom it is aimed."

— Joseph Stalin

Such was the insecurity on the part of the nation's leaders in the communist era that they herded all the successful, intelligent people of the day and sent them to Siberia. There was absolutely no resemblance to the freedoms that we enjoy in the West today.

As I lived and worked alongside the women in Moldova, it became very clear that they needed much encouragement; they needed to be told that they have value; that they could play a massive part in seeing the regeneration of Moldovan culture. Sadly, the women with whom I connected felt that they had nothing to offer. First and foremost, they were women, and they were treated very much as second class.

The culture is very slowly beginning to change, but it remains to this day, a male-dominated stronghold. Many men are alcoholics and treat their women really badly. Many suffer abuse at their hands and stay submissive and demoralised.

I felt very strongly that the women with whom I was interacting needed to be told how precious they were and how valuable they could be to society. I believe that they were and are pivotal in their roles to change the family dynamic from male dominance to a more shared care, equal status within the family. Of course, this would take time and much of what was being said was being heard for the very first time! To start this journey without the help and direction from Jesus would have been very foolish.

It was Jesus that they needed, His redemptive power and the freedom that brings to address their family situations and change mindsets forever.

Our annual conferences provided a safe place in which they could begin to realise their value for the first time. A chance to explore opportunities and to be encouraged to stretch their boundaries a little. It was a place where they could hear just how God felt about them and how much He loved them. That God wanted them to find their purpose, to walk in tune with His will and purposes and to experience the freedom that brings.

The joy and fulfilment that comes when we not only know our worth but we are also in the place where God wants us to be. Knowing the plans and purposes that God has for us is key to reaching our full potential as we journey daily in His presence. Our true worth in Jesus.

My time in Moldova was a great learning curve, and whilst the country was no longer under the rule of communism, the culture was still heavily influenced by those who had lived through that system and knew no other. To introduce something new was extremely difficult. However, gradually things are changing; a new generation is growing up not having experienced the communist regime, and suddenly, young people are becoming inventive and ambitious, many educated to degree level. This is resulting in many new businesses flourishing, people are again beginning to dream, and entrepreneurs are being born.

I dared to dream of hosting a national women's conference in Chisinau, the capital city of Moldova. I asked God if it was the right thing to do, and to be sure that I was doing the right thing, I said to God that I would invite a key speaker who was living in South Africa at the time. Her name is Margaret Stunt, if she was willing to come and was available on that specific date, then I would go ahead. Margaret has been a tremendous influence in my life for many years, the biggest encourager and "Jesus lover" that you will ever meet.

Her no-nonsense style and big, big faith was just what we were needing at the time. To my amazement, I had a very excited response from Margaret, my key speaker, who said she would be thrilled to come and speak to the ladies of Moldova! I knew from that moment; I was good to go!

The title was Women of Destiny, and it was to be held in a very smart hotel called the Leo Grand Hotel. This was a real upmarket hotel with a huge conference room decorated with beautiful chandeliers and mirrored walls. The room could hold 1,000 ladies, and I knew that I would need to fill it to cover the costs of hiring, lunch, and all logistical costs, etc.

It was a bit daunting at first, especially as I was a missionary with absolutely no money!!! However, one of my supporters, a wonderful gentleman called Glyn MacAulay, agreed to underwrite the budget, and that gave me the confidence to go ahead.

I knew that the ladies (especially from the villages) would never have been in such exotic surroundings, and so, I deliberately chose the most up-market hotel so that we could honour them with this "once in a lifetime" experience. The tickets were heavily subsidised to enable absolutely every woman to attend regardless of their income.

I worked with my dear friend and fellow missionary Charlotte Petersen from Denmark and developed a programme with a team of fabulous women from a charismatic Russian church in Moldova.

We contacted all the churches; hired buses to drive the women to the city, and brought Vera Kasovitch to speak from Hillsong church in Kiev, Ukraine, together with speakers from Canada and the UK.

We laid out a plush red carpet sprinkled with rose petals for the ladies to walk on as they entered the conference hall. We lined the carpet with men in dinner suits, and their job was to applaud every single woman that stepped on the carpet.

It was better than a night at the Oscars, with many women in floods of tears as they walked into this tremendous accolade. Here were young men honouring these ladies and touching the deep hurts and frustrations that they had been carrying from a deeply misogynistic culture.

We would marvel as hundreds of women answered the call to accept Jesus into their lives. Many running to the front of the auditorium, tottering in their high heels and miniskirts!

Miracles ensued as women were set free and released into their potential. We gave every single lady a beautiful journal that had been donated by Hillsong Church Kiev. Every lady was followed up by the local churches and encouraged to keep on, keeping on, connecting with the church fellowships and growing in their faith.

The miracle was that the dream of a national women's conference, (the first of its kind!) was realised. God had backed it; God wanted every one of those ladies for His Kingdom purposes, and He trusted me and a small team of people to do His bidding. Such a privilege to be His helper and such an enormous joy to see hundreds of lives transformed!

“The Lord Gives the Word in Power: the women who bear and publish the news are a great host”. Psalm 68 vs 11

Large and small groups of ladies gather regularly now to learn more of the love of God. There is such a hunger for the Bible, a hunger that we don’t seem to see any more in the West. Slowly women are beginning to walk in their freedom, hold positions in leadership and become the women that God has called them to be; that amazing desire that He injected into them before they were even born.

Just one of many wonderful testimonies….

I will close this chapter with a testimony from a woman who was saved but went home to a drunken husband who was aggressive and difficult, to say the least.

As she was praying about her situation, God asked her to write “post-it” notes of love and affection from herself and also the children. To tell her husband that he was dearly loved and needed, his family needed him. He was loved and needed to head up their family unit, to take his position.

The woman and her children covered the walls of their house with post-it notes of love, love, love so that no wall could be seen, only "post-it" notes of love messages.

The husband came home that evening drunk, as usual, and saw what the family had done. He began to read the love messages, and as he was reading, he broke into a hundred pieces, fell on his knees, and cried out for forgiveness. He met with Jesus that night and surrendered his life to Him. This couple are now, not only church leaders but are overseeing many churches across Moldova!

Such is the miraculous power that flows from our Heavenly Father!

Praise Him and Him alone for His abundant blessing, mercy, forgiveness, healing, and of course, for His MIRACULOUS Power!

Chapter 9

An invitation we couldn't refuse!

Tiraspol is the capital city of Transnistria, a Russian stronghold on the Eastern side of Moldova. Transnistria is part of the Republic of Moldova but maintains its Russian roots and culture and prefers to operate independently from Moldova as a whole.

There is a huge Christian church in Tiraspol that maintains links with the Christians in Moldova, particularly those who are part of the charismatic church movement.

Through the relationship with Charlotte and Johannes, Margaret Stunt, myself, Charlotte, and my daughter Samantha, who was visiting Moldova, received an invitation to their women's conference. Margaret was to be their key speaker, and we were her support team.

We were all very excited to be going on this road trip together, into the unknown. We all piled into my Shogun in Chisinau. I was nominated to drive as Charlotte was more nervous at the wheel, and I was very comfortable. However, there was a slight complication as I had lost my driver's license and was waiting for a replacement, so, legally, I should not have been driving. Charlotte had her license but didn't want to drive. This scenario was about to cause us several issues along the way.

We took the risk and set off, very happily, on our big adventure. We were all so excited; the volume of chatter in the car was immense. But, before we had even left the city, we were stopped by the police! I was very used to this as my car had a foreign number plate, so I was regularly stopped and asked to show my documents.

The policeman was very lenient as he discovered that I couldn't show him my license. He didn't believe my story that I had lost it and was waiting for a replacement. However, he said, that if Charlotte did the driving, he would let us off with no fine.

We changed places, Charlotte took the driver's seat whilst I jumped into the back seat. She drove around the corner and out of sight. I got back into the driver's seat, and off we went. Everybody was happy.

It was around a hundred and fifty kilometres to Tiraspol, so we all settled in for the drive, chatting away, as girls do and sharing fun stories, mostly about Jesus.

About a hundred kilometres into the journey, we came to a halt as a huge Russian tank was blocking our route. There were two uniformed soldiers with the tank, they were, fierce and quite adamant that we were not going to pass. The soldiers told us to get out of the car and questioned us as to where we were going.

Charlotte, who was Russian speaking, explained where we were going, but they were determined not to allow us to pass and suggested that we take the road through the villages. We really didn't have any choice, so even though this would lengthen our journey somewhat, we carried on taking the long way around. More than a little shaken from our ordeal.

We eventually came to a border crossing between Transnistria and Moldova and had to hand in our passports. It's never a comfortable feeling to hand over your passport to a stranger. It always raised the levels of anxiety somewhat. However, trusting it all to the Lord, we did as we were told and went from booth to booth as instructed. We shared the same information with each booth, were handed pieces of paper that no one understood, and did all that we could in order to pass over into Transnistria.

Thank God for Charlotte; without a Russian-speaking person, this task would have been extremely difficult. More than an hour had passed, and we were running out of time. Emphasising that we had a deadline and had to be at our destination by 6 pm and would now be late arriving. Charlotte decided to ask some questions, "Why is this taking so long?" "Where are our passports, and can we have them back tout suite?" or words to that effect.

Eventually, our passports appeared with all the appropriate stamps, and we were, once more, on our way.

Everything was beginning to be "plain sailing" until… disaster struck again! I had made a classic mistake. I inadvertently crossed a solid white line! ARGH! This just happened to be right in front of a road traffic officer who had just emerged from a traffic office that was in the middle of the roundabout. This office had two police officers inside who were responsible for monitoring traffic.

He immediately waved his baton and signalled me to pull off the road.

Now remember, I'm not supposed to be driving as I don't have a license. Charlotte handed me her license, which had her picture on it from a few years ago, so we sort of knew that it wouldn't wash. However, I brazened it out, was frogmarched into the little shack that was their office, and tried to convince them the picture was me!

I don't know to this day what possessed us to try, as Charlotte is from Denmark and is very blonde, 12 years younger than me, and I was brunette at the time. We must have been mad!

Whilst I was trying to explain the situation and getting nowhere, Charlotte walked into the office. The two police officers immediately recognised that it was Charlotte on the license ID and not me.

They couldn't understand why we would switch roles as Charlotte had the ID, but I was doing the driving; this was of great amusement to them. They kept saying, so you (meaning Charlotte) had the license but chose to be in the back of the car, and you (meaning me), who didn't have a license chose to drive. They seemed to be extremely amused by this tale.

The police officers were hysterical as they shook their heads, and one of them exclaimed, "zhenshchiny, zhenshchiny, zhenshchiny! My nikogda ne poymem zhenshchin" In English, "women, women, women! We will never understand women."

They then insisted, once more, that Charlotte got in the driving seat, and once more, we were on our way, once more, escaping a fine!

We finally made it to the church just in time for the conference. We all sat at round tables, and there was food provided, which was a very welcome sight. There were lots of fun activities, and eventually, they introduced Margaret, who, true to form, delivered a very powerful Gospel message, and many of the young women came forward to give their lives to Jesus.

We stayed at Pastor Uri's house that evening, and we all had dinner together. He had seven children, and I believe that several had been adopted. It was an amazing family, full of love, and a really beautiful time was experienced by all of us on that trip.

Our host suggested that we take a completely different route back, one which had a very simple border crossing which meant that we could show our passports through the car window and then be waved through.

The route home took half of the time that we had taken to get to Tiraspol. The whole trip had been one amazing adventure.

We marvelled at the way we were treated along the way. Usually, the Russian authorities are extremely harsh and very quick to arrest or issue a fine for the simplest of errors. We talked and laughed all the way home about how we had escaped arrest and escaped police traffic fines and how we had experienced miracle after miracle.

It was truly miraculous that the police officers thought we were just being "blonde" and, therefore, managed to escape all punishments. God constantly rescued us from the hands of the border police and the traffic police, who could have fined us a great deal of cash.

But the biggest miracle of all was to see a great host of ladies give their lives to Jesus that day. We had the result that we all passionately wanted to see. Hallelujah!

Chapter 10

The adventure continues…

And so, the adventure continues to this day. The goodness of God never ceases to amaze me. As I write this final chapter, I remember the most amazing trip Bill and I have just completed. We visited Melbourne, Tasmania, Sydney, and many towns on route. I could never have imagined the life which God had planned out for me since I gave my life to Him on 2nd November 1997. I will be eternally grateful to God and my bro, Eric, for praying me in; for having the faith to continue to believe for me, even when it seemed that I would never make his baptism service. All the odds were stacked against him. But for God, I would never have been present. God had other ideas; He can do what no one else can do.

My life continues to be an exciting adventure every single day, and my gratitude to my Heavenly Father is never-ending.

God continues to work His miracles in my life, here is yet another story of God intervention and loving kindness.

Whilst Bill and I were in Melbourne visiting his sister, Liz, and her daughter Catherine, I somehow managed to twist my back; not sure exactly what happened, but I do know that I was in excruciating pain. I had to brace myself every time I sat down, or I climbed into the car. Getting in and out of bed was a nightmare. I had developed a technique to ease the trauma, which consisted of a series of rolling movements until I was on my hands and knees on the floor and able very, very slowly stand up. And for that, I needed the help of Bill.

I had never experienced anything like this before and don't want to experience it ever again.

We had enjoyed an amazing time in Tasmania and were about to drive for five days from Melbourne to Sydney along the coastal road. The journey was long, and it would be six hours every day sitting in a car with a back problem. I had a sturdy cushion from Liz to support my back, but it was still very uncomfortable. I was wondering how I would manage.

However, I was determined that I wouldn't miss a moment of this incredible adventure. Liz dropped us at the car hire office, and we said our goodbyes. Bill helped me out of the car and I limped pathetically to the hire car office.

We filled in all the paperwork for the hire car, and the lady told us which bay to head to so that we could pick it up. When we saw the car, a large 4x4, we were alarmed that the front bumper had been badly damaged and not reported. Back we went to the desk to report our findings. After a considerable time and more form filling, the very pleasant lady we were dealing with said that we had been upgraded to a luxury model.

She said that we would really enjoy the ride in our "top of the range, Hybrid, Peugeot 508", particularly, as it had **all-electric, warming, and massage seats!!** I looked at Bill, and we both grinned; this was yet another miracle; God wanted me to travel in comfort. I had no idea that cars had built-in massage seats; it was pure heaven and kept me comfortable for the whole five days that we were in the car. By the time we reached the end of our five day drive, my back pain had completely gone, thanks to the incredible massages that I received along the journey every day.

Here we were, finally in Sydney, what a magnificent city. Hillsong Church Sydney had been on my bucket list for years, but I never thought I would actually be able to experience it. My dream came true the following Sunday. Bill and I were able to meet up with my dear friend Margaret and her husband, so we worshipped together at Hillsong. What an absolute privilege. Margaret Stunt had accompanied me on my journey in Moldova so many times. Her encouragements kept me going when things got tough, and to now be in Sydney, on her turf, enjoying worship at Hillsong together, was really special.

It didn't stop there; the following evening, we were taken to dinner in a "Windows on the World" restaurant at the Shangri-la Hotel. This was on the very top floor of the Hotel and overlooked the whole of Sydney Harbour. As you can imagine, the views were spectacular from Sydney Opera House to the famous Sydney Harbour Bridge and beyond. It was breath-taking and an incredible treat, courtesy of Fred and Margaret.

The adventure never stops; Bill and I enjoy every moment and will always be grateful to God that He brought us together. He has a plan for our future, and He will outwork His purposes through us both as we journey on.

I pinch myself every morning as I look around my beautiful home and remember where I came from. I arrived in Camberley with a suitcase of books and a suitcase of clothes, and here I am with everything I need, content and full of joy for the incredible journey that I am on.

In 2007, God stripped me of everything as I left to work on the front line in Moldova. Now,

He has returned to me, everything and more than I could ever have imagined. The journey was awesome; the adventure continues; my love for God, deeper and richer, every day and in every way.

Surely our God is the God of the miraculous! If we believe!

Psalm 34:8

Taste and see that the LORD is good; blessed is the one who takes refuge in him.

Epilogue

Following our marriage, I wanted to formalise our support for Moldova and to become an official conduit for funds that would help transform that nation. I was passionate that the work I had started should continue.

We both felt that we needed to be a recognised charity, and so we founded the Love Moldova Foundation.

Through the foundation, we support the girls shelter and residential business academy, which is the continued vision of Charlotte and Johannes. They are full-time missionaries in Moldova and have established many churches both in Moldova and in the Ukraine. Charlotte and Johannes also founded a rehabilitation centre for substance abuse victims. Their heart and passion for the nation is impressive, and we are cheering them on all the way, supporting wherever we can to enable transformation through their ministry and the Gospel of Jesus.

We continue to support Casa Helen, ensuring that all the needs are met. We are encouraged that we are able to send a Pastor to visit the ladies every few weeks, to pray with them, and to tell them about the love of Jesus. We hold regular services for the ladies and a small choir sings to them.

Leonid and Samantha Sandu (my eldest daughter and son-in-love) are also full time missionaries and partners with the Love Moldova Foundation. They have recently invested their lives in a small church in a rural village in Moldova, and they are heavily involved in the mayor's office in Ungheni, where they distribute humanitarian aid. Through the Love Moldova Foundation, they are able to heavily subsidise those families who are on the poverty line. Often paying their fuel bills and giving them food boxes.

A particular need at the moment is for children with Autism and physical disabilities. These children have no support from the state. Their families often have to sell their homes to pay for medical support and equipment. Samantha is in the process of developing a vision for a sensory centre for these children, together with a room where parents can meet up and share their experiences.

Love Moldova sponsors an annual women's conference called LIMITLESS, which celebrates women's extraordinary potential. We hold the conference in the UK and then take the whole package to Moldova; complete with our key speakers. We believe in empowering and releasing women into their God-given Destiny. We want to develop leaders for the future and to encourage every young woman to invest in their nation and to take the lead to influence others too.

We have recently sponsored two young people through bible college and are looking forward to watching their journeys unfold.

If you would like to see more of the work of Love Moldova, please do visit our website.

As I sign off this chapter, we are heavily involved in supporting the Ukrainian refugee crisis across Moldova; providing homes for refugees; food; clothing, etc. All of our efforts wrapped up in compassion and loving kindness. We are so grateful to the amazing partners in Moldova, constantly on the front line, loving and caring for the lost, the last and the least. Always ready with a hug and a smile and a place to stay, rest and be fed. They are the real heroes of The Love Moldova Foundation.

So, let's finish with worship to our magnificent God.

1 Chronicles 29

11.Yours, LORD, is the greatness and the power
and the glory and the majesty and the splendor,
for everything in heaven and earth is yours.
Yours, LORD, is the kingdom;
you are exalted as head over all. Wealth and honor come from you;
you are the ruler of all things.
In your hands are strength and power
to exalt and give strength to all.
13 Now, our God, we give you thanks,
and praise your glorious name.

www.lovemoldova.foundation.

REGISTERED CHARITY #1174960

love
MOLDOVA
FOUNDATION

Ingram Content Group UK Ltd.
Milton Keynes UK
UKHW022141150623
423525UK00007B/54

9 781916 596917